The Tunnel

Virginia King

Illustrated by Brian Harrison

Revised USA Edition © 2003 Published by Scholastic Inc.
By arrangement with Reed International Books, Australia Pty Ltd.

The Tunnel
0-439-64861-0

Text copyright © Virginia King
Illustrations copyright © Brian Harrison
Momentum Program © Reed International Books, Australia Pty Ltd., 2003

Printed in China by QP International Ltd

10 9 8 7 6 5 4 3 2 1   04 05 06

Contents

Chapter One

Harmless Lies

Dean knew he wasn't normal. He'd known for some time. Ever since that night years ago. He tried hard not to think about that night.

His friends didn't know. They thought he was just like them. It was hard work pretending all the time. But it would be much worse if they found out.

When his friends asked him to do things with them, like stay overnight, Dean made sure he was always too busy. He pretended that his father was always making him stay at home and do chores.

Over the years, his best friend Benny had decided that Dean's dad must be really mean and strict. Of course this wasn't true, but it helped Dean to create this impression. He knew that if he spent too much time with his friends, they'd soon find out about him.

"Oh, come on, Dean," said Benny, for what seemed like the hundredth time. "We're just going to throw a basketball around. Your dad would let you do that, wouldn't he?"

Maybe that would be okay, thought Dean. He could play some basketball, as long as he didn't stay too long. "Er, what time?" he asked.

"Come over to my place about four o'clock. Then afterward we could watch a video."

"I can't stay after dark," Dean blurted out, a little too quickly. Then he decided that the risk was too great, so he said, "Sorry, I can't come."

"I don't get it," taunted Josh, the new boy. "If you're scared of walking home in the dark, couldn't your dad pick you up?"

Dean felt his breath catch in his throat. He wouldn't think of that night, not now! He forced his face into a silly grin, which he hoped looked relaxed. He wanted to speak, but he knew his voice would shake, so he kicked a pebble instead.

"No, that's not it," said Benny, unknowingly coming to the rescue. "His dad won't let him go out."

"Too bad," said Josh. "It's great at Benny's place. His mom makes the best chocolate brownies."

Dean watched Josh and Benny walk off without him. As usual he felt left out. But he also felt relieved. Dean knew that if his friends ever saw him after dark, they'd never speak to him again.

As usual, he wandered home by himself, making sure he was well inside before darkness fell. It would be winter soon, when it got dark early. He dreaded those months of short days, when he had to scurry home like a crazed rabbit and hide inside where no one could see him.

Chapter Two

After Dark

When he got home, he went straight into the kitchen to do his homework. He grabbed a glass of milk and sat down at the table with his books.

"I wish you'd work in your room, Dean," said his mother. "I'm sure you'd be able to concentrate better."

"But I like it here," said Dean, trying not to sound like he was pleading. He had to stay here in the bright light, like he did every night. "I work better with people around me," he added, trying to convince her to let him stay.

His mother sighed. "You've always been a strange one," she said. "Your father and I need absolute quiet to work. That's why we got you that great desk for your room, and you never use it." She always said stuff like that.

Yeah, I'm strange all right, thought Dean, wishing as he did every day that he was like everyone else. "You could sell the desk," he suggested. It would be a great relief to him not to have her mention it all the time. And not to have it staring at him every time he went into his room.

"No, we won't sell it," said his mother. "You'll probably use it when you're older."

Yeah, thought Dean, when dogs can talk and pigs can fly.

Dean tried to concentrate on his homework. It was always better if he didn't look out the window as the sun started to set. His mother usually closed the curtains then, and if she didn't, he'd do it himself.

Without looking out, of course. It wasn't so bad when she was there with him. It was when he was alone that things were the worst.

When his dad came home, Dean was busy reading a book about volcanoes. They were doing a project at school. He didn't like looking at the pictures that were taken under the ground. There were amazing tunnels called lava tubes, which were formed when a river of lava cooled quickly on the outside, creating a tunnel as the hotter lava inside flowed away. He was fascinated to read about them, but he quickly turned away when he came to the pictures. They made him shudder.

"You're amazing, Dean." His dad had just come in and was messing Dean's hair as he walked past. "All my friends at work complain that they can't get their kids to come inside and do their homework. And I have to tell them that I can't get my boy to get his nose out of his books!"

Dean waited for the next sentence. He'd heard it so often.

"I really think you should spend more time out in the fresh air, Dean. It's not healthy to stay cooped up inside all the time."

"Yeah, Dad. When I finish this volcano project."
Dean always had an excuse. Sometimes, it felt like his
whole life was an excuse.

"Okay," said his dad. "When the project's finished,
invite some of your friends over after school. They can
stay the night, or I can drive them home when I get
back from work."

"Yeah, sure, Dad," Dean said, feeling that familiar
tightness in his throat, knowing it would never happen.

Dean moved his books off the table so they could
eat. Dean ate carefully, trying not to think what was
going on outside the kitchen curtains.

Inside it was bright. But outside ...

"We're going on a school trip soon," he said, trying
to keep his mind distracted.

"Where to?" asked his dad, his mouth full of food. Dean noticed that his dad was always pleased when he thought Dean was going to do something adventurous.

"Some sort of rafting. Down a river, I think."

Now his dad was really interested. "That sounds great," he said. "Where's the river?"

"I can't remember," said Dean, truthfully. "But it's some kind of water rafting."

"White-water rafting!" exclaimed his dad. "That's great. You get really wet, but it's fantastic fun. I did it years ago, when I was at school."

"Yeah, the teacher seems to think we'll enjoy it. I'll be bringing home all the information in a few days."

"Aren't you nervous?" asked his mother, surprised that Dean would be interested in going on something that sounded scary to her. She'd always thought her son was rather timid. Well, for the last few years anyway.

"Nervous?" asked Dean, incredulously. How could anyone be scared of anything in broad daylight? "No, it's during school time. I'm not nervous."

"What's the time of day got to do with it?" asked his mother. After all these years, Dean had managed to keep his "problem" a secret from her.

Dean had to think fast. "Well, you know, all the kids and teachers will be there," he improvised. "That means it can't be scary."

"I guess so," she said.

Afterward, Dean helped to stack the dishwasher and then went back to his books, trying not to think of bedtime. As always, it came too soon.

Chapter Three

A Nightly Ritual

"You've done enough work for tonight," Dean's mother said from the living-room door. "Time for bed."

"Okay," he said, knowing that he had to do what he struggled with every night. Go to his room alone.

He walked through the living room on his way to the stairs, keeping his breath as steady as he could. His father had dozed off in a chair. "Good night, Dad," he managed to call and heard a grunt in reply.

There was a light switch at the bottom of the stairs that he turned on gratefully. At least the stairs were bright.

Up he went. Step by stiff step. Closer and closer to his door. As he did every night, he opened the door just a crack to reveal the darkness beyond and quickly flicked the switch just inside the door. His room was flooded with light, but that wasn't enough. As he inched through the doorway, making sure his parents couldn't see this bizarre ritual, he turned his back on the windows and stepped backward. He knew he was holding his breath. His whole body was shuddering with suppressed panic. But he couldn't breathe again until he'd done it.

It was as if his whole life stood still, waiting for the moment when it would be over. Without looking, he stretched out his arm behind him and grabbed the curtain cord. Then, with a sudden jerky movement that threatened to pull the whole curtain down, he pulled the cord—and closed the curtain! As he collapsed on the bed, he felt his arms and legs go limp. He felt the air rush back into his lungs. He stopped himself from crying out with the sheer relief of it. He'd done it again. He'd closed out the darkness.

Chapter Four

The Fear

The fear had started that night five years ago when Dean was only six. He was going to Kids' Klub one afternoon each week after school, while his mother was studying. She usually picked him up on her way home, but this time she'd asked his dad to get him. It was wintertime and Dean waited outside Kids' Klub under the tree, like he always did. At first there were other children playing in the yard, but gradually their parents came for them. Dean waited and waited, but his dad didn't come. Little by little it got dark. The teacher didn't see him standing in the shadows. She climbed into her car and drove off. Dean didn't know that he should call out to her. He just stood like a statue and waited.

Kids' Klub was held in a small building that stood all by itself at the end of a quiet street surrounded by trees. The trees looked different in the dark. Big and creepy, with long arms instead of branches. There were strange noises, too. Noises of the night. Hooting and scratching and rustling. It was hard to keep standing there, waiting for his dad.

Dean wanted to run and hide, but when he looked back at the big black windows of Kids' Klub, they looked like huge mouths, waiting to swallow him. Once he saw some glowing eyes looking at him from the shadows and he cried out, but there was no one there to hear him. That was when the shuddering started. And the tightness in his throat.

By the time Dean's dad got home that night, saw the accusing look on his wife's face when he came in alone, and then drove all the way back to Kids' Klub, Dean's whole body was stiff and shuddering. His eyes were frozen and staring. It wasn't just the cold. It was the fear.

For days afterward, Dean couldn't speak. And he would never go back to Kids' Klub.

That was five years ago, and Dean's parents didn't know that their son was still terrified of the dark. It had taken him several months to start behaving normally again. Gradually he had learned to hide his fear. And they had stopped worrying.

Dean had tried to talk himself out of it. In his mind
he knew that the night couldn't really hurt him. After
all, it was just the sun going down! But all the talking
didn't help. Whenever he saw the darkness, he saw
those windows at Kids' Klub. He saw again those dark,
sinister mouths waiting to swallow him up. His whole
body started to shudder and his throat became so tight
that he couldn't speak. Each time it happened he
recovered, but he was worried that eventually the
darkness would turn him to stone.

19

Chapter Five

Blackwater River

"Will your dad let you go on the rafting trip?" Benny asked.

"Sure," said Dean, forgetting to keep up his dad's reputation. "He thinks it sounds great. He's so excited, I think he'd like to come himself!"

"Your dad sure is weird," said Benny. "I can't figure him out."

"Me neither," said Dean, deciding this was the best way to handle it. "Anyway, I'm going."

"I can't wait to wear a wetsuit again," said Josh. "They're cool."

"You mean cold," joked Dean. "And wet."

Benny laughed, but Josh just shrugged.

"I wonder why it's called the Blackwater River," said Benny.

"My dad says when you go through rapids in a river, it's called white-water rafting," said Dean, "So, maybe the water in this river is deeper. That could make it look black."

"That could be it," said Benny, losing interest.

"Yeah, or it's probably just a name," said Josh, "to make it sound scary."

"It doesn't sound scary to me," said Dean.

"I didn't mean that I'm scared," said Josh. "I'm not scared of anything."

The class gathered at seven o'clock in the morning, ready for the bus ride to Blackwater River. There was a lot of chattering and nervous laughter as everyone tried to show their friends that riding the rapids wasn't such a big deal. Josh was explaining loudly to everyone what it was going to be like, as if he was an expert.

Dean was bored with his boasting. "Have you been white-water rafting before, Josh?" he asked in front of everyone.

"Well, er, not like this," admitted Josh.

"What then?" Dean asked, hoping to show him up.

"Well, I've been canoeing," said Josh.

"In a fast-flowing river?" Dean persisted.

"Pretty fast," said Josh.

Everyone groaned. The last thing they wanted to hear was advice from a show-off.

"Just wait till you get in the river, Dean," hissed Josh. "If you get scared, I won't help you."

"Good," said Dean, trying to sound braver than he felt. "I won't need your help."

"We'll see," said Josh, grinning.

The teacher hadn't told them very much about it. "Part of this trip is a surprise," he said, mysteriously. "And there'll be lots to discuss afterward."

Now they were all on the bus, and as they got closer to their destination, there was a strange silence of anticipation among the group, mixed with a little fear.

"I wonder what the surprise is," whispered Benny.

Dean could hear the tension in Benny's voice. "It won't be long until we find out," he replied, feeling strangely calm. At least, he wasn't scared of everything. Just one thing.

When they arrived at the staging area, they were met by a man called Guy. "My team will help you get into the wetsuits and the other gear, and then I'll explain what's going to happen," he said. "Please follow all our instructions carefully."

Dean and the other kids pulled on the wetsuits that Guy had provided.

They were told to leave their shoes on.

"Swimming in shoes. That's weird," said Benny.

Everyone seemed to be talking in subdued voices. They could feel the excitement.

"Probably to keep out the cold," suggested Dean. "And maybe there are rocks."

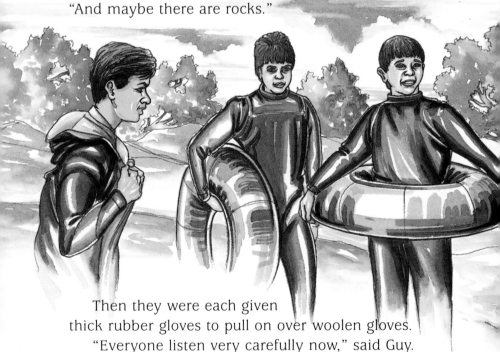

Then they were each given thick rubber gloves to pull on over woolen gloves.

"Everyone listen very carefully now," said Guy.

The strangely dressed group gathered around.

"We all look like penguins or something." Benny giggled.

"Quiet now," said Guy. "It's important that all of you hear my instructions. The way this works is that each of you will be given a tire tube. Climb inside your tube like this." Guy demonstrated, stepping into the tube and pulling it up to his waist.

Josh snorted. "It looks like a hula hoop. I thought we'd be using canoes. Tubes are for babies who can't swim."

The others waited for Guy's response. Tire tubes did seem silly. Was this the surprise?

"The tube is the best way to travel down this river," continued Guy. "It's too rocky for canoes. Canoes are for safer, calmer rivers."

Several of the others turned and smirked at Josh.

"The tube is much more maneuverable and gives you more control," said Guy. "It keeps you afloat and protects you from the rocks at the sides. The reason you're wearing shoes and gloves is also for protection, so you can push yourself off the rocks if you need to. I need to warn you that you're going to get very wet!"

Some of the kids cheered. Now they were impatient to get moving.

They all stepped into their tubes and Guy led them down to the river.

Dean was amazed at how narrow it was. And fast. The dark water was flying past. In the light it looked like a black satin ribbon. Blackwater River, he thought.

"You'll go into the river one at a time," Guy was saying. "I'll tell you when to jump, so you're not too close to the person in front."

They all lined up. Somehow, Dean ended up right behind Josh. At least he's not behind me, Dean thought.

They were just about to begin, when Guy raised his voice again. "And when you get to the waterfall, enjoy it!"

Chapter Six

Riding the Rapids

Guy pushed the first boy into the water, followed by a redheaded girl who decided to scream. After that, everyone screamed as they jumped in. It was a great release of all their tension. Everyone screamed except Josh. He's too brave to scream, thought Dean with a chuckle.

And then it was his turn. Into the dark, swirling river he went. With the first plunge he almost went under, but then he remembered to keep his arms well out over the tube, with it firmly up under his armpits.

At least, I'm all wet, he thought. Now I can enjoy myself.

Dean could see Josh turning around in front of him and waving rudely at him. He seemed to have his usual smirk on his face. Dean ignored him and looked up at the high sides of the river. It's like a kind of canyon, he thought. And then he knew what the surprise was. It's flowing through an old lava tube, he thought. It probably used to be a long tunnel. I'll bet the teacher is going to ask us after the trip!

And then he looked up ahead and saw what he should have predicted. It was the part of the lava tube that hadn't worn away. It loomed up in front of him. A yawning mouth. The dark mouth of a tunnel. Dean craned his neck, trying to see daylight through the opening. But there was none.

There was nothing he could do. The river was carrying him along and there was no turning back. He was about to enter a long, dark tunnel. A tunnel so dark that he couldn't see daylight at the other end. How long could it be? He tried to remember what he'd read in the volcano books. Sometimes lava tubes could be several miles long!

Dean could feel his body start to freeze up, and it wasn't because of the cold. All he could think of was the dark mouth up ahead. Just like the windows in Kids' Klub. A dark mouth about to swallow him up.

On and on the water carried him. Closer and closer. And in front of him the mouth of the tunnel got bigger and bigger. Soon he would be inside and there would be no more light. Just the dark.

He could feel his eyes getting wider as the fear overcame him. He just stared straight ahead as the tunnel swallowed him. And he stopped breathing.

Through the dark entrance the black water carried him, into a tunnel that might have no end, into the dark that would turn him to stone. He tried to breathe, but as usual, his breath had caught in his throat. His whole body stiffened with his familiar reaction to his fear. He saw the sides of a long tunnel closing in on him. And then he thought of his friends, of Josh just up ahead. What if they see me? he thought.

He didn't want them to see the fear that he had kept a secret for so long.

But by then it was too dark to see anything.

Dean could hear the water dripping down the walls and could see nothing but the dark. He lost all sense of time. There was just the water and the darkness and his own rigid body, which now was beginning to shudder.

Just when he thought that the dark would indeed take him, he heard a noise. It was a sound so terrifying that it jolted his attention away from himself. The sound was much worse than anything he was feeling inside. It came from just up ahead. And then he recognized it. It was the sound of Josh screaming.

Chapter Seven

Over the Edge

The next thing Dean knew he was screaming himself.

The water had carried him over a cliff. He was falling. Falling, falling, falling, into complete blackness, accompanied by the echoing sound of his own voice. Now his ears were full of the thunder of crashing water. He could feel it foaming down his back. He flailed his arms about to keep himself upright. When he hit the deep water below, he thought he was going to slide under, but the tube kept him up and stopped him from swallowing mouthfuls of water.

He stopped screaming.

Then Dean noticed something. He was breathing. He was in the dark, and he was breathing normally. And his body wasn't stiff anymore. His limbs were relaxed, going with the flow of the water.

Dean noticed that the water seemed to be flowing slower now. The thunderous noise of the waterfall was far behind him. There was a peacefulness here. He was able to stretch back against his rubber tube and look around him. He looked up. At first he thought he was outside again, because he could see stars. But that didn't make sense because it was still early in the day. Then he realized that the lava tube had opened up into a cavern with a high roof, and the ceiling of the tunnel was covered with little pinpricks of light: glowworms.

Dean glided along, fascinated. He had read about glowworms, but had never seen them, because he was

always hiding at home away from the dark! Now the river was carrying him along, and he could lie back and gaze up at the gallery of tiny lights. With a surprise, he realized that he was enjoying himself.

There was another sound, something that disturbed him. At first, he couldn't figure out what it was. But it was so persistent that at last he knew. It was a whimpering noise. Josh was crying.

Dean wasn't sure what to do. Should he try to catch up with him, or should he leave him to cry alone? He didn't spend much time debating. He found that if he kicked his legs, he could propel himself forward. And Josh seemed to have slowed down. He was getting closer. When Dean came up behind him, he saw that Josh was clinging to a rock.

"Scary, isn't it?" said Dean in a loud voice, pretending not to notice Josh's sobs. "Let's do the last part together."

Josh seemed relieved. Because of the glowworms, it wasn't so dark, and Dean saw Josh nod. Dean grabbed at Josh's tube and pulled him away from the side. Together they let the river carry them on through the tunnel.

Dean knew that when you're scared it helps to have someone take your mind off it, so he chattered on about the glowworms, until the tunnel opened out into daylight. Then, when he saw the landing area up ahead, he let go of Josh's tube.

Guy and his team had stretched a rope across the river. Josh grabbed the rope, and then Dean grabbed it himself. Slowly they pulled themselves to the river bank.

As they climbed out, Guy threw blankets over their shoulders and said in his hearty voice, "So, how was it?"

"Fantastic," Dean blurted out. He was surprised to hear the eagerness of his answer. He didn't even have to think about it.

"Would you like to do it again?" asked Guy. "The bus is here to take you back up river."

"Yes!" said Dean, again not thinking.

"Now you know why we call it blackwater rafting," chuckled Guy, "instead of white-water rafting."

Dean laughed. His dad would enjoy the joke, too.

When he looked at Josh, he was looking deathly pale.

"I'm not feeling well," Josh said to Guy. "I think I must be sick from the bus trip."

"Sure," said Guy, nodding his head in understanding.

More kids were arriving at the rope, and the bank was becoming crowded.

Some were saying they'd like to do it again, and others were saying no way!

"Not me," said Benny. "It was great," he added, "but once is enough!"

Everyone noticed how quiet Josh was. "He's feeling sick from the bus trip," Dean told them.

Josh pulled Dean aside and whispered, "Thanks."

"Thanks for what?" asked Dean, wanting to pretend that nothing had happened.

"You know."

"It was nothing," said Dean, shrugging his shoulders.

Then Josh looked around and murmured, "You won't tell anyone, will you?"

"Nothing to tell," said Dean, and he patted Josh on the shoulder.

Then he walked over to Benny. "Can I come over to your place this afternoon?" he asked. "We'll probably be too tired to play basketball, but we could watch a video. And then over the weekend, maybe you could stay at my house."

"Sure!" said Benny, looking a little puzzled. "What about your dad?"

"He's cool," said Dean, pleased to be able to tell the truth at last.